For more information address Disney Press,
114 Fifth Avenue, New York, New York 10011-5690

ISBN 978-1-4231-7409-7

Printed in the United States of America

First Edition

10 9 8 7 6 5 4 3 2 1

For more Disney Press fun, visit disneybooks.com

G658-7729-4-13172

School Dance Madness

By Calliope Glass

Illustrated by Davide Baldoni, Stefania Fiorillo, and Fabio Pochet

DISNEY PRESS

New York

"**A**pples? Check. Pineapple? Check. Plums? Check," Daisy said out loud to no one in particular.

Standing in the produce section of the grocery store, she looked down at the shopping list in her hand. There were still a lot of things left on it.

"Carrots, broccoli, green beans, whole wheat bread, peanut butter, oatmeal, and . . . **VegGummables?!**"

Daisy had heard of VegGummables—gum balls that came in flavors including beet,

cucumber, and eggplant—but she didn't think
anyone actually *liked* them!

"Mrs. Flamingo is kind of strange," Daisy
muttered to herself, "but vegetable-flavored gum?
That's weird even for her."

Mrs. Flamingo was the art teacher at Mouston
Central. She had hired Daisy to pet-sit for her
sugar glider, Sugarplum, a few weeks ago. And
apparently she thought Daisy did a really good job,
because ever since then, she had been paying Daisy
to do random tasks.

Last week, Daisy had helped Mrs. Flamingo—
who wasn't very good with computers—put five of
her handmade sugar slider sweaters up for auction

on the DownByTheBay auction site.

Daisy wasn't quite sure why a sugar glider would need a sweater, but that was beside the point. She liked running errands and doing chores for Mrs. Flamingo. It was nice to feel responsible, and the extra money was going into her wet suit savings fund. Soon she would be able to surf in style!

Daisy started looking for the gum balls.

Aha! Daisy plucked a bag of VegGummables off the shelf. She tossed it in her shopping basket. Maybe once she'd been paid she'd get a treat for herself . . . a treat not flavored with asparagus, radishes, or squash!

"Boo!"

"Wak!" Daisy jumped a mile. She turned around. It was her friend Leonard.

"You scared me!" she scolded him.

"Sorry, Daisy," Leonard said, smiling. He looked down at the contents of her basket and glanced up with a confused expression on his face. "I thought you were allergic to pineapple," he said.

"I am," Daisy replied. "I'm shopping for Mrs. Flamingo!" she said proudly.

"Nice! I was dropping off the recycling," Leonard replied. "And running some other errands." He was carrying a huge stack of books. "I have to return these to the library."

Daisy squinted at the books. One of them was called *Computer Simulations for Beginners*.

Leonard was a bit of a nerd. But he wasn't afraid to be himself, and **Daisy admired that about him.**

Chapter 2

Leonard was glad he'd bumped into Daisy in the grocery store. He hadn't seen her for a while—it seemed like she was always at the beach surfing! Also, he'd been spending a lot of time in his home laboratory (his bedroom), creating a new virtual reality skateboarding game.

Leonard **loved science and inventing things.** He won first prize in last year's science fair for building an elaborate alarm clock that tickled your feet to wake you up. To Leonard, science was just as much fun as skateboarding and watching monster movies.

"Why are you reading *Computer Simulations for Beginners*?" Daisy said to Leonard as they walked through the store together. She pointed at his stack of books.

"I'm inventing an all-immersive experience for skateboarders," Leonard said. "Basically, you put your own skateboard on a stationary support structure. Then you put on these goggles I'm designing that allow you to visit any skate park in the country. As you 'skate' around the park, you lean on your board as you would in real life, and sensors on the support structure communicate with the goggles to alter your course."

coolest.

"Can you repeat that in English?" Daisy said, completely confused.

Leonard laughed. "Never mind," he said. "So are you going to the dance tonight?"

"Blech, no way!" Daisy said.

Daisy hated school dances. Mostly because she thought the music was awful, but also because she always felt pressure to go with a date. Plus, tickets for couples cost seventy-five dollars, while tickets for singles cost fifty. Daisy thought it was incredibly unfair.

"You?" she asked Leonard.

"Nope," he said. "I just got a few monster movies from a discount DVD Web site and I'd much rather watch *Slime Three: The Slimening* than go to some lame dance."

Leonard also hated school dances, mostly because he thought the food was awful, but also because he, too, always felt pressure to go with a date.

"*Slime Three?* Wow!" Daisy said. "I heard that one's even better than *Slime Two: Son of Slime.* And *Slime Two* ended with such a cliff-hanger!"

"I know!" Leonard exclaimed. "Doctor Itzelweiner was just about to throw the switch on his Goopinator machine, which would cover the island of Mousehattan in key lime pie filling!"

Daisy shared Leonard's love of monster movies. It was one of the reasons Leonard liked hanging out with Daisy. (But just as a friend. Not in a mushy way or anything.)

"Ooh!" Daisy said, clapping her hands together. "We should watch it together! I was just planning to watch repeats of *Lana Wyoming,* but this will be a million times better!"

"Sure," Leonard said. "Come over tonight, and we'll get slimed!"

"It's a date," Daisy said. "I'll bring some candy."

Leonard eyed her shopping basket suspiciously. "Just as long as it's something other than VegGummables!" he said.

"Are you sure?" Daisy said, holding up the candy. "Three VegGummables contain the full recommended daily amount of vitamin C!" she joked.

Leonard laughed. "No, thanks," he said. "I had some orange juice with breakfast, so I'm all set. See you later!" He grinned and waved good-bye to Daisy. Then he headed off to finish his errands.

Chapter 3

Ding, dong!

Daisy rang Mrs. Flamingo's doorbell and tried to catch her breath. The supermarket was nearly two miles from Mrs. Flamingo's house, and **the groceries were heavy!**

I thought I was in great shape from playing so much tennis! Daisy thought as she panted. She shifted the bag of groceries so it rested on her hip. It seemed to get heavier by the second. Maybe I need to do a bit more upper-body training, she thought.

17

She resolved to add push-ups and pull-ups to her morning routine.

Finally, Mrs. Flamingo came to the door.

"Oh, dear!" she said. "Come in, Daisy. Your arms must be tired!"

"I think I got everything on the list," Daisy told her.

"Good!" Mrs. Flamingo said. "Even the VegGummables? I know they can be hard to find."

"Yep!" Daisy said proudly. "There was only one

bag left, so I was lucky to get it! They must be delicious."

More like gross, Daisy thought to herself.

"Thank you!" Mrs. Flamingo exclaimed. "I try to stay away from sweets for Sugarplum's sake, but I cannot resist these gum balls. I just have to keep them locked up, because if he were to get into them, he would fly into a sugar craze!"

Daisy knew exactly what Mrs. Flamingo meant. When she took care of Sugarplum, he had gotten loose inside an ice cream parlor and devoured every treat in sight! He had even sailed right into Abigail's milk shake, causing it to spill all over her.

That part hadn't been so bad. In fact, it had been pretty hilarious.

Even now, Sugarplum was staring at the VegGummables **like they were double-fudge brownies.**

"I believe I owe you ten dollars for today's job," Mrs. Flamingo said. She rummaged around in her purse. "Still saving up for that surfboard?"

"No, I bought it a few weeks ago with my pet-sitting money!" Daisy said. "Now I've got my eye on a **SnazzyShredder wet suit.** But I might have to spend a little bit of this and get some candy for me and Leonard to share tonight." Licorice, she thought to herself. *Or peanut-butter cups. Or taffy. Or gummy worms!*

"Oh! Is Leonard your date for the dance?" Mrs. Flamingo asked. She waggled her eyebrows at Daisy.

No way! Daisy thought. She considered Leonard to be a friend. And she liked him a lot. But she didn't *like* like him. Even if she did *like* like him, there's no way she'd go to a school dance with him.

Daisy shook her head. "Dances aren't really my thing."

"I'm surprised!" Mrs. Flamingo said. "An outgoing girl like you—not a fan of dances?"

"I like rock concerts better," Daisy said. "Or basketball games. Or monster movies.

"In fact," Daisy went on, "I'm going over to Leonard's house tonight to watch a monster movie instead of going to the dance."

Mrs. Flamingo's eyebrows shot up.

"A *monster* movie?!" she said. "What a coincidence!"

Daisy was confused. Mrs. Flamingo didn't exactly seem like the vampire-and-werewolf type. **"You like monster movies, too?"** she asked.

"Oh, no, no," Mrs. Flamingo replied. "I'm afraid of my own shadow. Even those TwiFright movies give me the jitters."

What?! Daisy thought. *Waking Spawn* was *so* not scary. She had actually laughed during

the scene when all the other girls in the theater were burying their heads in their boyfriends' shoulders.

Now, *Zombie Hunters 4: Even More Zombies, that* was a scary movie.

Mrs. Flamingo continued. "It just so happens that I take Zumballet classes with Ms. Labrador, who owns the movie theater downtown. She gives me tickets to all sorts of things."

Mrs. Flamingo fished around in her pocket. "**And do I ever have a surprise for you!**" she said.

Chapter 5

Mrs. Flamingo held up two tickets. "Ms. Labrador gave me these passes to the monster movie festival tonight at her theater!"

Daisy gasped. She had heard about Monster Mayhem, but when she went to the box office, it was completely sold out!

"Now," Mrs. Flamingo said, "**my nerves aren't up to this sort of thing.** But I bet yours are!"

"**Wow!**" Daisy said. This was awesome! "For me?"

"Well, *I'm* definitely not going to use them," Mrs. Flamingo said. "I have my knitting club tonight, and it's my turn to bring snacks. I've been working on a recipe for the past couple weeks, but I realized at the last minute that I was missing a few ingredients. That's why I'm so glad that you were able to go to the market for me!"

I bet she's making artichoke and squash casserole with broccoli-carrot sauce on top, Daisy thought. But she wisely kept this opinion to herself.

"No sweat," Daisy said, before she remembered that the errand actually *did* cause her to sweat quite a bit! "I would have carried twice that many groceries twice that far for a chance to go to Monster Mayhem!"

"Then it looks like this arrangement worked out perfectly for both of us!" Mrs. Flamingo said.

"Thanks, Mrs. F.!" Daisy gushed. "I can't wait to tell Leonard that we're going to the film festival. **He'll be stoked!** They are playing deleted scenes from *Slime Two* that didn't even make it onto the special edition DVD!"

"Well, you kids enjoy yourselves," Mrs. Flamingo said. "Don't get *too* scared!"

Daisy hopped down the porch steps. She had to hurry—she was supposed to meet Minnie at **Duck Duck Juice for lunch** at twelve thirty, and it was already twelve twenty-five. After lunch, Daisy would call Leonard and tell him the great news about the tickets.

It was going to be an **awesome night!**

Chapter 6

Leonard was almost done with his errands. "Library," he muttered to himself. "Then home. Then tonight—monster movie with Daisy!"

Leonard liked having plans. He liked knowing what to expect. He did not like surprises.

As Leonard walked, he thought about the new books he was planning to borrow from the library. One that he was especially excited to read was called *When You Get the Blue Screen of Death*. Leonard loved bringing broken computers back to life. He considered himself to be a **modern Dr. Frankenstein.** Except without the monster.

The route to the library took Leonard right by Mrs. Flamingo's house. Oh, he thought, this is where Daisy was going when I saw her at the grocery store.

Sure enough, as Leonard walked by Mrs. Flamingo's house, there was Daisy, heading down the steps! He was about to call out to her, when . . .

"What are those?" he muttered to himself. Daisy was holding two tickets.

Leonard felt his stomach lurch. What if those were tickets to the dance? Maybe Daisy had decided to go after all and she was going to cancel their plans for tonight!

It was certainly possible. Daisy was a very cool girl, and Leonard knew at least three guys at Mouston who had crushes on her. Did one of them ask her to the dance?

Leonard squinted hard at Daisy's hand.

OMG! She was holding two **tickets to Monster Mayhem.** He couldn't believe it. He'd been trying to get a ticket for *months*!

Daisy's gotta give me one of those tickets, Leonard said to himself. She's just got to!

That's our thing!

Okay, **calm down,** he thought. Leonard took a deep breath. She's probably already planning on giving me one, he pointed out to himself. Daisy's a good friend. And we were going to watch a monster movie tonight anyway!

But then Leonard remembered that Daisy was having lunch with Minnie. What if she asks

Minnie to go to Monster Mayhem? he thought.
They are BFFs, after all!

Maybe if he got to Duck Duck Juice before
Minnie arrived, he'd have a chance to talk to
Daisy. But he had to return his library books first!

Chapter 7

Daisy loved Duck Duck Juice. She loved their smoothies and their sandwiches. And they made incredible chocolate-macadamia cookies. But the thing she loved best about Duck Duck Juice was that it was her and Minnie's *spot*. It was their **favorite hangout,** and that made it special.

They went to DDJ—as she and Minnie called it—so often that the waitresses even knew Daisy's and Minnie's names. And what they usually ordered!

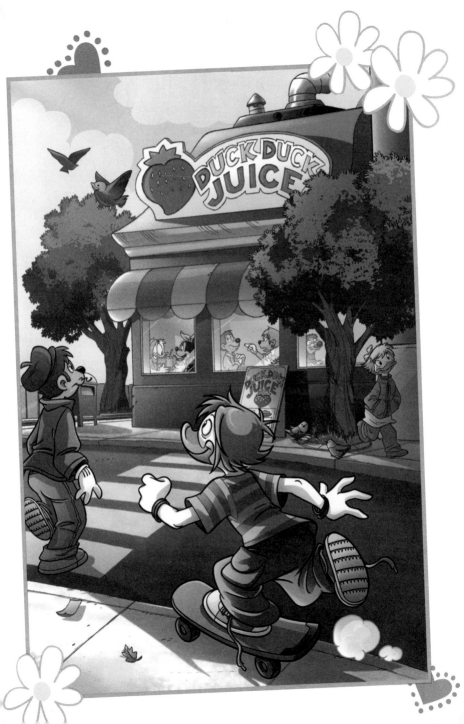

Daisy plopped down at their usual table.
Minnie was already there.

"**Hey, BFF!**" Minnie said.

"Hey back atcha!" Daisy said. "Minnie, you'll
never guess what I have!"

She couldn't wait to tell Minnie the news
about Monster Mayhem.

"A pretty dress to wear to the dance tonight?"
Minnie asked.

"No," Daisy said, kind of annoyed. Minnie
knew she wasn't going to the dance. But that
didn't stop her from pestering Daisy about it.
Unlike her best friend, Minnie adored dances,
and she was hoping that Daisy might change her

mind about going.

Daisy waved the tickets at Minnie.

"I've got **two tickets to Monster Mayhem** tonight!" she said. "I'm so excited!"

Minnie wrinkled her nose. "How is that better than a dance?" she asked. Minnie loved that a dance gave her the opportunity to make a pretty dress, wear that pretty dress, and then scope out her classmates' pretty dresses.

"**I love you, Minnie,**" Daisy said. "But just because we're BFFs doesn't mean we have to agree about everything! I love awesome, scary movies, and you love dumb, boring school

dances." She grinned at her friend, teasing.

"**Oh, shush,**" Minnie said. "Well, I'm happy for you, I guess. So, are you taking Leonard with you? I mean, he loves monster movies, too."

"You bet!" Daisy said. "I just haven't told him yet."

"That's awesome! You get to watch *ScrodZilla Versus the Giant Squid*, and I get to wear the dress, I designed for the dance," Minnie said.

"Oh, Minnie, I wish I could see you in it!" Daisy exclaimed. She knew that Minnie was going to be a famous fashion designer one day.

"Well, I'm sure that my parents will take lots of pictures before I leave for the dance," Minnie said.

"If it's anything like the dress you designed for the Homecoming fund-raiser," Daisy said, "I'm sure everyone at the dance will love it."

Minnie smiled. "It's going to be a *fantastic* night for both of us. **I can't wait!**"

Chapter 8

Leonard zipped along on his skateboard. He had felt so anxious about finding Daisy that he had completely abandoned his plans to take out *When You Get the Blue Screen of Death*.

Fixing computers could wait. He had to get to Daisy before she had a chance to give Minnie the second ticket to Monster Mayhem!

When Leonard arrived at Duck Duck Juice, he peered into the window.

Rats! he thought to himself.

Daisy and Minnie were already inside and sitting in their usual booth.

But there was still a shred of hope. Maybe Daisy hadn't mentioned the movie festival to Minnie yet. He leaned in closer to the window, thinking that he might be able to hear their conversation.

There wasn't much noise on the street (and Minnie's voice was pretty high-pitched), so Leonard had no trouble hearing Minnie say, "It's going to be a *fantastic* night for both of us. **I can't wait!**"

A chill went down Leonard's spine. (Even chillier than the chill he got the first time he saw *Zombie Hunters 3: Zombies Galore*.)

He was too late.

Daisy was taking Minnie to Monster Mayhem—not him.

This was *not* going the way Leonard had hoped. Not at all!

"I know, I know!" Leonard heard Daisy say. "You wouldn't miss it for anything in the world!"

"I didn't even know Minnie liked monster movies," Leonard muttered to himself. "But Daisy gave her a ticket anyway. This is the absolute worst! Everything is ruined."

Leonard's mom was always telling him not to be so dramatic. But this was a dramatic situation! His chance to see Monster Mayhem was gone forever. This was even worse than the time he took second place in the science fair. Worse even than the time he waited in line overnight for the iDrone 8 and they ran out before he could buy one.

Leonard stomped off in disappointment.

Chapter 9

Inside Duck Duck Juice, Daisy listened with a fond smile as Minnie went on about the dance.

"I've been working on my dress nonstop!" Minnie said. "Originally, I was going to do something inspired by fairy tales."

"**Mmm-hmm,**" Daisy said.

"I thought about using Cinderella as a model and designing a ball gown with a full skirt," Minnie said. "I also considered doing an A-line silhouette, just like Aurora's dress in *Sleeping Beauty*."

"But then I changed my mind when I found out that the theme of the dance was 'Magic Under the Stars,'" Minnie went on. "I knew what I had to do!"

"What was that?" Daisy asked. She liked it when Minnie got all fired up about stuff. It was fun to watch her wave her hands around enthusiastically.

"I created a dress," Minnie said, pausing dramatically, "inspired by the night sky."

Daisy was a very literal duck. "You mean it's black?" she said.

Minnie laughed. "No, silly!" she said. "First, I came up with a fun, modern design," Minnie went on. She showed Daisy a drawing of the dress. "And then I cut stars out of white satin."

"Wow," Daisy said. She was impressed. Minnie was a terrific designer, and she kept getting better and better. The dress was stunning.

51

"Unfortunately," Minnie continued, "my sewing machine broke before I had a chance to sew the stars on. So after we finish lunch, I'm heading to the costume shop at school so I can use the drama department sewing machine."

Chapter 10

Leonard ended up at the park. Normally, skateboarding would help him feel better, but he was so upset and distracted, he was afraid he might board right into a hot dog cart.

Miserable and disappointed, Leonard wandered around for a while, dragging his feet.

Ugh. Life was just so unfair! If only he hadn't bumped into Daisy at the grocery store, none of this would have happened. He would

be home, reading *When You Get the Blue Screen of Death*.

Finally, he plopped down on the swings. "I can't believe it," Leonard said.

The little kid who was swinging next to him stared at him. He sucked on a lollipop.

"She invited Minnie instead of me," Leonard told the kid. "But I'm Daisy's monster-movie-watching friend! That's what our friendship is all about!"

The kid just continued to stare at him in silence.

This seemed to encourage Leonard to continue. "I just don't get it! Daisy told me once that she took Minnie to see *Creature with the Pink Balloon* and Minnie hid her eyes the entire time! Even during the credits!"

Leonard was really on a roll now.

"I bet Minnie only pretended to be excited about Monster Mayhem," he said. "She's probably dreading it! I would actually be doing

her a favor by offering to go in her place!"

Suddenly, an idea came to him. Leonard leaped off the swing with a burst of energy.

"Wait a minute!" he said. "Maybe I can fix this. Daisy already invited Minnie, but if I asked her nicely . . . if I reminded her about all the good times we've had, watching scary movies . . . and subtly suggest that Minnie might not actually want to go . . . maybe she would give the ticket to me, instead."

The little kid pumped his legs and swung higher.

"But it's tricky," Leonard said. "Daisy and Minnie are BFFs. I don't want to mess with that. I've seen what happens when they fight, and it's not pretty."

He looked at the kid. "What do you think?"

The kid didn't say anything.

But Leonard didn't need any encouragement. "I should practice. That way when I see Daisy,

I won't screw up asking her for the ticket."

The kid stared at him and let his swing slow down to a stop.

"Oh, hello there," Leonard said. He pretended the little kid was Daisy. "I was just looking for you. Daisy, I wanted to ask you something. It's about tonight. I know that you have two tickets to Monster Mayhem because I saw you leaving Mrs. Flamingo's house. I also know that you're planning to take Minnie with you. But . . ."

Chapter 11

After the BFFs finished lunch, Daisy pulled out her cell phone and tried calling Leonard. But it went straight to voice mail.

Hmm, she thought. His phone must be off. **I'll just have to go find him!**

Daisy biked all around town, looking for Leonard. She checked the technology section of the library, the video games store, and even Leonard's favorite taco stand. But he was nowhere to be found.

Where could he be? Daisy wondered. What

was Leonard talking about when I last saw him? Daisy asked herself. The library, computer programs, skateboarding. . . .

That's it! she thought. He must have gone skateboarding in the park!

Daisy pedaled as fast as she could, bouncing with excitement to tell him about the Monster Mayhem tickets.

Finally, she heard his voice coming from the playground area. She hopped off her bike and started walking toward Leonard. He was talking and waving his hands. It almost looked like he was practicing for a play or something.

"That's odd," Daisy said to herself. "Minnie's the local theater fan, not Leonard." But he was definitely rehearsing a speech. And his audience was the most annoyed-looking six-year-old Daisy had ever seen.

As she got closer, Daisy could hear exactly what Leonard was saying.

"Daisy," he said. "I wanted to tell you something. It's really important to me."

"Huh," Daisy said to herself. "That's odd—he's practicing a speech for *me*?"

Daisy knew that it wasn't right to eavesdrop, but she was curious to hear what Leonard was saying. So she hid behind a bush to make sure he wouldn't see her.

"Tonight," Leonard said, "tonight, I want to go with you to—"

Then he stopped. **"I just can't do it!"** he said. "I'm too chicken to ask her!"

Daisy couldn't believe it. It sounded like. . . .

"Leonard wants to ask me to the dance?!"
Daisy said to herself. "That's crazy! He hates
dances as much as I do. Why would he do that?"

Unless . . .

"Leonard has a *crush on me!*"

Oh, boy.

Chapter 12

"**I**'m such a coward!" Leonard said.

Now Daisy felt *really* guilty for listening in on Leonard's speech. So she didn't stick around to hear the rest of it.

Making sure to be very quiet, she snuck off down the park path. The last thing she wanted was for Leonard to notice her! She would have to explain why she had been spying on him, and he would probably launch into his dance invitation. **It would be a disaster!**

Daisy hardly knew what to think.

"Sure, I like Leonard," she said to herself. **"But not *like* like. Not like *that*."**

It had never occurred to Daisy that Leonard might like her like that. They'd known each other forever. They'd been friends since they were little. They watched monster movies, studied for science, and played "Duck Duck Dance Battle" together. And Leonard had never said anything about liking her.

A terrible thought occurred to Daisy. "Earlier today . . ." she said to herself. "When I saw Leonard at the grocery store. We agreed to watch the movie tonight. And I said, **'It's a date.'** I didn't mean to give him ideas! I didn't mean it was *literally* a date!"

Maybe this was all her fault.

All Daisy wanted was to enjoy Monster Mayhem with her friend! And now everything was *hopelessly* complicated.

"Why did I have to say *date*?" she wailed. **"Me and my big mouth!** If only I hadn't run into Leonard at the grocery store this morning. None of this would have happened!" Daisy kicked at a stone.

Chapter 13

"Ouch!" There was a yelp from the other side of the bush. The stone Daisy kicked had hit someone! Between her frustration, and the fact that she had been practicing corner kicks in her backyard in preparation for soccer tryouts, Daisy had kicked the stone pretty hard.

She hadn't thought it was possible to feel any worse, but now she felt absolutely terrible.

"Sorry!" Daisy yelled. She hurried over to see who it was.

"Mike?" Daisy said, surprised. He was in her math class.

"Yep, that's me," Mike said. He rubbed his head. "You must be really good at soccer," he said. "You kick hard."

"Well, I have gone through three goal nets in the last two weeks." Daisy realized that she had gotten completely off-topic. "But that's beside the point! I'm so sorry about your head!" she said.

Mike just shrugged.

He must be really upset, Daisy thought.

"Do you want me to get you some ice?" she offered. "There's a QuackieMart around the corner. . . ."

"**No,**" Mike said, sounding sad. He tossed a bread crumb to the pigeons. Daisy thought he seemed awfully distressed. More than the average person might be after getting pelted with a pebble.

Plus, Mike was usually a pretty cheerful guy.

"Is something else bothering you?" she asked. "Besides the goose egg that's quickly developing on your forehead?"

"**It's embarrassing,**" Mike mumbled. "You'll laugh at me."

"I promise I won't," Daisy said. "I just booted a rock at your face. The least I can do is listen."

Daisy didn't know Mike very well, but he seemed like he needed someone to talk to.

"It's about tonight's dance," Mike said. "I really want to go."

"So, go to the dance," Daisy said. She didn't see what the problem was.

"I want to go with a girl," Mike said. "Like, on a date. But I'm too chicken to ask anyone! I've been trying to work up the courage for weeks, but every time I approach a girl, I lose my nerve. I tried calling, because I thought it would be easier on the phone than face-to-face, but as soon as I hear a voice on the other end, I hang up!"

Daisy was starting to get really fed up with this whole situation.

"This dance is causing more problems than a sugar glider in an ice cream parlor!" she yelled.

"Huh?!" Mike said, very confused. "What

are you talking about?"

Daisy explained about running into Leonard in the grocery store and asking him if he wanted to watch a monster movie. "But then Mrs. Flamingo gave me two tickets to Monster Mayhem," Daisy continued. "And when I went to find Leonard to surprise him with the second ticket, I overheard him practicing this big speech. I hid in the bushes so I could listen in secret, and it was just awful! He's going to ask me to the dance!"

Mike looked even more confused. "Why is that so terrible?" he asked. "Don't you like Leonard?"

Chapter 14

"I like Leonard just fine," Daisy said. "I just don't *like* like Leonard. I don't want to hurt his feelings by saying no, but I also don't want him to get the wrong idea. Because he's my friend, and that's all I want him to be. **Ugh, what do I *do*?**"

Mike thought hard for a few minutes. Finally, he said, "You know, considering my problems asking someone to the dance, I'm probably not the best person to be giving you advice. But I've got an idea. Here's your solution. Go find

Leonard and ask him to the dance."

"**What?!**" Daisy had never heard a dumber idea in her whole life. "Mike, I don't think you've been listening."

"No, no," Mike said. "This is perfect. Ask him to go to the dance with you—as *friends*. Just as friends. Tell him you changed your mind, and instead of watching a monster movie, you'd rather go to the dance after all. And you think it would be fun for you two to go as buddies."

"Huh," Daisy said. "And that way . . ."

"That way, he gets to go to the dance with you," Mike finished. "But on your terms."

"**That's a really good idea,**" Daisy said. "Thanks, Mike."

Of course, this meant that Daisy couldn't go to Monster Mayhem. That was a bummer. But if it meant saving her friendship with Leonard, she was willing to sacrifice a few zombie movies. Maybe they could even catch the tail end of the deleted scenes if they left the dance early. But then she would have to wear her dance clothes to the movie theater, and she would be way overdressed for a monsterfest. . . .

"**Uh-oh,**" she said. An even bigger problem had just occurred to her. "**I need a dress and the dance is tonight!**"

Mike shrugged. "You have lots of dresses,"
he said. "I've seen you wear them."

Daisy rolled her eyes. *Boys.* "I can't wear an
old dress to a school dance," she explained. "The
whole point of going to a dance is wearing a
new dress."

"Seriously?" Mike said. "I don't get girls at all."

Daisy pulled out the contents of her pockets.
She had the ten dollars Mrs. Flamingo had given
her that morning, plus some change from her
lunch with Minnie. But even with the twenty
dollars she had saved for the wet suit, she
wouldn't have enough.

Chapter 15

"There's no way I can buy a formal dress for thirty dollars!" Daisy said. "Especially so last minute! All of the good deals will be gone, and the sale racks will be cleaned out!"

But Mike wasn't really listening. He was staring at Daisy's hand. "Are those tickets to Monster Mayhem?!" he asked excitedly.

"Yeah," Daisy said sadly. She had been so thrilled about going. And now the tickets would go to waste.

"I've got another idea," Mike said. "How about I buy them from you? There's no way I'll be able to work up the courage to ask someone to the dance, and it would be nice to have something to do tonight so I don't sit home and mope!"

Daisy felt a pang in her stomach at the thought of letting the tickets go, but she really needed the money. She made her decision.

"Perfect!" Daisy said. "I'll have enough for a dress!"

This might turn out okay after all, Daisy thought as she handed Mike the tickets.

Mike smiled halfheartedly as he gave Daisy his allowance money. "Well, this isn't exactly how either of us pictured tonight going, but it's not too bad, right?"

"No, I guess not," Daisy said. "But now I have to take off."

"Okay. Good luck with everything, Daisy," Mike said.

"Thanks! Have fun tonight, Mike!" Daisy said.

And then she hurried away—she had to find Minnie! They had some shopping to do . . . fast.

aisy burst through the doors of the school. She knew she'd find Minnie in the costume shop behind the auditorium putting the finishing touches on her dress for the dance.

With any luck, Minnie would be done and willing to sacrifice some precious getting-ready time for a quick trip to the mall. The best dresses would definitely be gone by now, but Daisy wasn't too picky. Just as long as she didn't have to wear a shawl, she would be fine. Daisy hated wearing shawls.

"**Minnie!**" Daisy cried as she burst into the costume design room. "I need your help! I have to go to the dance! With Leonard! And I don't have anything to wear!"

Minnie looked up from her worktable. She gaped at Daisy.

For a minute, Minnie's mouth moved without any words coming out. When she recovered her ability to speak, Minnie said, "I'm sorry. I must have misheard you. It sounded like you said you're going to the dance with Leonard."

"I am!" Daisy wailed. "It's the longest story *ever*. But the short version is: I need a new dress!"

"**Can you help me?**" Daisy asked. There was no time to spare!

"Well," Minnie said slowly. "Actually, yeah."

"Great!" Daisy said. "Where should we go? The department store? The boutique? The vintage shop? I know it's a long shot, but we might be able to find something at—"

"We don't have to go anywhere," Minnie said, interrupting her friend.

"Huh?" Daisy said. She didn't understand.

Chapter 17

"I've got a dress for you right here," Minnie explained.

She pointed at a dress hanging in the corner. It was pink, with stars and lace that shimmered softly in the dim light.

"You can use mine," Minnie said. "I'm not going to the dance, so I don't need it." Minnie's voice broke on the last two words. Daisy could tell that her best friend was on the verge of tears.

Daisy's jaw dropped. "What?!" This day was getting stranger and stranger. "Why not?"

Minnie looked like she was trying very hard not to cry. "I've called all the boys I can think of," she said. "And they're all busy! I don't have a date, Daisy. And I can't go alone—I just can't!"

Minnie couldn't hold her tears back any longer. She burst into sobs and hid her face in her hands.

Daisy hugged her friend tight. "Oh, Min," she said. **"I'm sorry. That's awful.** And how is that even possible? A million boys have crushes on you!"

Minnie sniffled. "I guess I just waited too long! I was so excited about my dress," she said. **"I spent all this time working on it."**

Daisy knew that Minnie could be a bit of a perfectionist. When Daisy had starred in the school production of *Romeo and Juliet,* Minnie had remade her dress about fifteen times!

Minnie picked the dress up and looked at it sadly. "I was so wrapped up in the dress that I

forgot to get a date."

Daisy felt awful for her friend. She knew how much dances meant to Minnie.

"I can't just wear your dress," Daisy said. "You should be wearing it."

Minnie smiled sadly at her friend.

"No," she said. "You're my BFF. If I can't wear it, then you should definitely wear it."

"Really?" Daisy said. Minnie was being so nice, but Daisy just didn't feel right about taking her friend's dress. "You worked so hard on it, Min!"

"So someone should wear it," Minnie said. She was smiling for real now. "Daisy, stop being so stubborn. You have a date to the dance. Now you have a dress, too. Enjoy it!"

"I don't know. . . ." Daisy said.

"This way my beautiful design won't be wasted!" Minnie said. "When you step onto the red carpet—erm, into the gym—and they say, 'Who are you wearing, Daisy?' you can tell them,

'Minnie Mouse Couture!'"

Daisy grinned. "Okay, you win."

"**Great,**" Minnie said. "Just let me make a few adjustments and it's all yours."

"And Minnie," Daisy said as Minnie began unzipping the dress, "someday you will wear one of your own designs on the red carpet, and the photographers will shout, 'Who are you wearing?!'"

Minnie smiled. Her BFF could always make her feel better.

Chapter 18

After Minnie had taken Daisy's measurements and put some pins in the dress, she encouraged Daisy to go find Leonard.

Daisy was nervous.

Leonard was her friend, and now that she knew he *like* liked her, she was scared of hurting his feelings. But at the same time, she had to ask him to the dance in such a way that he wouldn't think it was a date.

When did my life get so *complicated*? Daisy thought as she left the school.

Daisy headed back to the park. Leonard tended to get wrapped up in drama, so she figured he might still be there, practicing to ask her out.

"**Right again,** Daisy," she muttered to herself when she saw Leonard. He still looked tense. About as tense as Daisy felt!

"Hey!" she yelled. "Leonard! My friend! Old buddy, old pal!"

Ooh, I hope I'm not overdoing it, Daisy thought after the words escaped her mouth.

"Hi, Daisy," Leonard said. "That's weird, I was just going to look for you. Listen, I have something I just have to ask you."

No! Daisy had to head him off.

"Let me go first!" she said. This was so *awkward*. And Leonard looked a little offended. But she plowed ahead.

"Uh," Daisy said, "so, you know, about tonight. . . ."

"**Yes!**" Leonard interrupted her. "Tonight! That's just what I wanted to talk to you about."

"Wait—" Daisy said. This was getting out of her control! "Not so fast!" But Leonard interrupted her again.

"I know this is awkward," Leonard said, talking fast and stuttering a little. "B-b-but, I saw you outside Mrs. Flamingo's house with the tickets to Monster Mayhem, and I know that you already promised it to Minnie, but **I really, really, really, really want to go!**"

gotta talk!

"Hold on," Daisy said. *"What?"*

Daisy's head was spinning.

"I need a do-over on this whole day," she said to Leonard. "But first, can you just repeat that for me?"

eonard looked as confused as she felt. "I want your second ticket to Monster Mayhem," he said. "After I saw you leave Mrs. Flamingo's, I followed you to Duck Duck Juice and I listened to your conversation with Minnie. I know that she's your best friend, so of course you would ask her to go with you. . . ."

"Huh?" Daisy was in shock. She was about to scold Leonard for spying on her and Minnie, but then she realized that she had done the same thing to him.

Leonard shuffled his feet awkwardly. "It's just, well, I remembered the time you took Minnie to go see *Creature with the Pink Balloon,* and she hid her eyes the entire time!" he said. "So I'm pretty sure that she wouldn't like Monster Mayhem." He grinned hopefully. "And I know I would!"

"Why would I give Minnie a ticket to a monster-movie festival?" Daisy asked.

"Whoa, now I'm confused," Leonard said. "Back up a second. If you didn't come here to cancel our plans for tonight, what were you about to tell me?"

Daisy felt as though she had just, in the nick of time, managed to stop Doctor Itzelweiner from throwing the switch on his Goopinator and covering the entire island of Mousehattan in key lime pie filling.

"Oh," Daisy said, giggling nervously, "it's not important. You wouldn't believe me anyway. You should drop it. Let's change the subject. Say, what a pretty tree that is!"

I can't believe I thought Leonard had a crush on me! she thought. He was probably practicing to ask me for the Monster Mayhem ticket!

This just **kept getting more and more embarrassing.**

Leonard smiled. "Come on, Daisy," he said. "Now I'm curious."

"Well . . ." Daisy said. **"Okay, but it's so dumb."**

She told him about how she overheard him in the park, how she assumed that he was going to ask her to the dance, how she sold the Monster Mayhem tickets so she could buy a dress. . . .

"Wait, you thought I had a crush on you?" Leonard asked. Then he burst out laughing.

Daisy snorted. It was sort of funny, now that she came to think of it. "I know," she said. "I can't believe it either."

"There's something I don't get," Daisy said.

"Hmm?" Leonard asked.

"Why on earth did you think I'd given Minnie the other ticket? While we were at lunch, all she could talk about was her dress for the dance."

"Oh," Leonard said. He blushed. "I overheard her saying how excited she was for tonight. I just assumed she meant that she was going to Monster Mayhem."

Daisy laughed. "Well, you were right about one thing: Minnie hates monster movies!" she

said. "Plus, she's been planning for this dance for, like, months. She even sewed her own dress!"

"**What a relief!**" Leonard said. "Now that we've gotten this whole situation cleared up, we can go to Monster Mayhem after all!"

Daisy felt her stomach sink. "No, we can't," she said.

Leonard did a quick rewind of Minnie's explanation. His eyes widened. "Because *you sold the tickets to Mike*," he said.

Daisy thought fast. Maybe, just maybe—Yes. She was a genius. She had a plan. She was going to save the day.

"There's still time," she said to Leonard. **"Trust me on this. I've got it all worked out."**

Chapter 21

Daisy filled Leonard in on her brilliant plan. "It might just work!" Leonard said.

"It *will* work," Daisy corrected him. "But only if we run!"

Daisy and Leonard tore out of the park. It was a good thing that Daisy had been jogging every morning to prep for soccer tryouts—the theater wasn't exactly around the corner. Leonard had a hard time keeping up with her!

"What if he's already gone in?" Leonard asked Daisy as they ran. Except it sounded more like "What" *pant* "if" *pant* "he's" *pant* "already" *pant pant* "**gone in?**" As they turned the corner onto Main Street, he managed to gasp, "The show starts at seven and it's already six fifty-eight!"

"Trust me," Daisy said. "Mike is late to math class almost every day. He's not exactly the punctual type."

Sure enough, just as they rounded the corner, they saw Mike walking ahead of them.

"Mike!" Daisy yelled. "We need to talk to you!"

Daisy skidded to a halt in front of Mike. He looked completely confused. Behind her, Leonard panted, catching his breath.

"**What's going on?**" Mike asked.

"Mike, you can go to the dance!" Daisy said. "Right now! I have a date for you!"

"Really?" Mike said. He couldn't believe what

he was hearing. "Are you pulling my tail?"

"No way!" Daisy said. "I'm completely serious! And she's going to be wearing an amazing dress, so you'd better head home and change your clothes."

"I don't get it," Mike said. "How did you find someone to go with me?"

"It's a really long story," Daisy said.

"Yeah," Leonard added. "A really long and complicated story."

"Okay," Mike said, still looking confused.

"But first you have to give us the Monster Mayhem tickets back," Leonard said.

Mike raised his eyebrows.
"**Wait a second.** I thought the
two of you were going to the dance!"

Daisy and Leonard laughed.

"There was a ginormous misunderstanding,"
Daisy explained. "But there's no time to go
into the details. You have to get to the dance—
and fast!"

"All right . . ." Mike said, handing over
the tickets. ". . . Who's my date?"

"It's Minnie!" Daisy said, returning Mike's
allowance money.

"*Minnie* Mouse?" Mike asked. He looked
amazed. "Minnie doesn't have a date to
the dance?"

"I know," Daisy said. "It's your lucky day. Now go home and comb your hair, put on a tie, and get yourself to school. The dance starts in half an hour!"

Mike's expression changed from confused to shocked. He was so shocked, in fact, that he wasn't moving. He just stared at Daisy like she had two beaks.

"What are you waiting for?!?" Daisy said. "Get a move on!"

Mike came back to his senses. "I just can't believe you got me a date with Minnie Mouse! I've had a crush on her since kindergarten!"

"You can thank me later," Daisy said. **"Now scram!"**

"Did you catch your breath yet?" Daisy asked Leonard.

"No," he wheezed.

"Too bad!" Daisy said. She grabbed his hand and pulled him into a run. "Because we have no time to spare!"

They bolted down Main Street, took a right onto Knowalot Lane, and sprinted the last few yards to Mouston Central. By the time they reached the entrance, Daisy was practically dragging Leonard by the hand.

Daisy had déjà vu, running through the halls of Mouston School again, just as she had an hour earlier.

Had it really only been an hour ago that she was planning to go to the dance with Leonard? It seemed like weeks!

Just as Daisy suspected, Minnie was right where Daisy had left her, in the costume shop. She was measuring out a length of green fabric.

"Minnie!" Daisy yelled as she burst in. **"Stop right there!"**

"Daisy," Minnie said. "I know you don't like shawls, but it's supposed to be pretty chilly tonight, so I'm making one to go with my, er, your dress. It should only take a few min—"

Daisy interrupted her. "Put down the fabric!" she yelled, "and listen to me!"

Minnie looked stunned, but she put down the fabric.

"You're not going to believe this," Daisy said, "but I've gotten everything worked out, finally. Leonard and I aren't going to the dance. We're going to Monster Mayhem. Which means I don't need your dress. Which is good, because you need it. Because you have a date for the dance."

"With Mike!" Leonard added. His breathing had finally returned to normal.

"I . . ." Minnie said, overwhelmed. "The who in the what, now?"

Daisy explained as quickly as she could.

"We just sent Mike to go home and change," Daisy said to Minnie, "so you should do the same. The dance starts in twenty minutes!"

"Daisy," Minnie said, as reality began to sink in, "I don't know how to thank you!"

"Just go and have a wonderful time!" Daisy said.

Chapter 23

innie couldn't believe what a strange day it had been. So many mix-ups!

"This is why people need to communicate better," she said to Mike over the loud music in the school gymnasium. The deejay was playing "Beauty and a Tweet" by Justin Beakber. It was one of Minnie's favorite songs.

"What?" Mike said, yelling at the top of his lungs.

Minnie shrugged. Oh, well.

She smiled up at her date. Mike looked

handsome in his suit and bow tie.

Minnie had had a crush on him since kindergarten, but she had been too embarrassed to ask him to the dance. It was turning out to be a pretty great night. And she felt like a movie star in her dress!

Had it really been just an hour ago that she thought she was going to miss the dance? It seemed like weeks!

"WANNA DANCE?" Mike shouted.

"YES!" Minnie yelled back. Now that *was* communication.

Minnie and Mike did the Quackarena, ate snacks, and chatted, er, yelled, with their friends.

Minnie got dozens of compliments on her dress, and a couple of girls even asked her to make their gowns for the Spring Formal.

"Minnie," one of them said, "I bet your designs will be on the racks at Quacks Sixth Avenue before you graduate from college!"

Minnie was glowing.

Finally, the music quieted down. It was time to announce the king and queen of the dance.

The class president got up onstage and took the microphone from the deejay.

Minnie held her breath. These types of competitions were usually popularity contests, so

Abigail almost always won. She hoped this time would be different.

"And the king and queen of the dance are . . ."
Mike squeezed her hand.

The class president opened an envelope and read the piece of paper inside. "Mike and Minnie!"

Minnie squealed happily. This was the best dance ever!

After they'd gone up to the stage and been crowned, Minnie got out her phone.

"Come on, Mike," she said. "Let's

send a picture to Daisy and Leonard!"

They posed together, and Minnie raised her phone and snapped a picture.

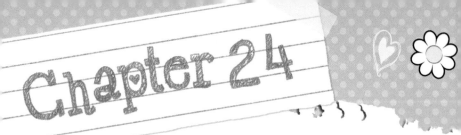

Meanwhile, on the other side of town:
"Grar! Hork! Slorp!"

The lights were dim in the movie theater.
Terrible monsters rampaged across the screen.
Luckily, Daisy and Leonard had only missed the
previews. Leonard had even purchased a green
sweatshirt with a googly-eyed–alien hood from
the souvenir stand in the lobby. He looked pretty
nerdy, but Daisy liked that about him.

Not *like* liked him, just to be clear.
Bzzz!

Daisy's phone vibrated. She looked down to check it. Next to her, Leonard leaned over.

"Is everything okay?" Leonard whispered.

"More than okay!" Daisy whispered back. "**Check this out!**"

"Looks like everyone's having a good night," Leonard said, looking at the picture of Minnie and Mike in their crowns.

Daisy held out a bag of candy to Leonard. "VegGummable?" she offered.

"Ugh!" Leonard said. He looked completely grossed out. Daisy laughed.

"**Just kidding!**" she said. "They're gummy worms."

Leonard dug in. "Do you think that monster looks like Sugarplum?" he asked Daisy, pointing at the screen.

"Nah," Daisy said. "**Sugarplum is scarier.**"